THOMAS
THE TANK ENGINE & FRIENDS
™

MILLENNIUM ANNUAL 2000

£5.99
UK only

Contents

Britt Allcroft's Thomas the Tank Engine & Friends
Based on The Railway Series by The Rev W Awdry
© Britt Allcroft (Thomas) LLC 1999

THOMAS THE TANK ENGINE & FRIENDS is a trademark of
Britt Allcroft Inc in the USA, Mexico and Canada and of
Britt Allcroft (Thomas) Limited in the rest of the world.
THE BRITT ALLCROFT COMPANY is a trademark of
The Britt Allcroft Company plc

Published in Great Britain in 1999 by Egmont World Limited,
Deanway Technology Centre, Wilmslow Road, Handforth, Cheshire SK9 3FB
Printed in Italy   ISBN 0 7498 4286 5

Slow Down, Thomas!

Thomas the Tank Engine is very proud to have his own branch line. He works really hard to make sure that everything is just right. He fusses around his coaches, Annie and Clarabel, and hurries them along so that he always gets his passengers to the station on time. He always makes sure that parcels and packages are delivered on time, too. He just hates being late, and enjoys rushing around keeping himself busy.

One day Thomas had an extra busy time.

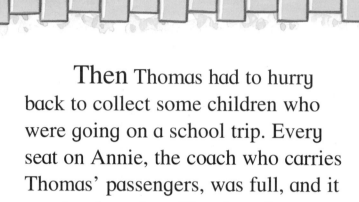

First, he took the men who work at the quarry to meet up with Toby and Henrietta so they could take them to work for the day.

Then Thomas had to hurry back to collect some children who were going on a school trip. Every seat on Annie, the coach who carries Thomas' passengers, was full, and it was hard work pulling her along.

Next, Thomas took Clarabel, the coach who carries goods as well as passengers, right to the end of the line. Clarabel was packed with parcels and boxes and packages. But Thomas' driver found that some had been left behind!

"Peep, peep!" said Thomas. "No problem!" and he steamed all the way back up the line to collect them. Thomas is a clever little engine, and he can travel backwards as well as forwards, but going backwards is hard work.

There was no time for a rest before Thomas had to steam back to meet the quarrymen, to take them home again.

"Well done, Thomas," said his driver when he took Thomas back to the shed for the night. "You've worked really hard today."

"Peep," said Thomas, but he sounded tired, and his peep was much quieter than usual.

Every night, the engines talked about what they had been doing. Thomas always enjoyed hearing about their adventures and telling his. But that night he yawned as Edward talked about how he had shunted the trucks around the yard. He could hardly stay awake.

Kind old Edward noticed how tired Thomas looked.

"You're such a busy little engine, Thomas," he said. "You should take it easy sometimes. Don't rush around so much. Rushing around is why you get into so many scrapes. You'll still get your jobs done if you go a bit slower, and you won't tire yourself out."

But Thomas didn't want to listen to Edward's advice.

"I like being busy," he said. "Going fast is good fun. I know you mean to be kind, Edward, but you don't always know what's best, you know. Not for me, anyway."

Henry agreed. "Thomas is right," he said. "It's fun being a really fast engine, just like me."

"Going fast can be fun," said Edward, "but your speed makes you upset sometimes, doesn't it, Henry? And rushing about has even made you ill." Henry had to agree that that was true, but Thomas still didn't like Edward's advice.

"Well, I'm not like Henry," said Thomas cheekily. "I never get tired and I'm never, ever ill. I like going fast, and I like being busy, so there!"

But the next morning Thomas still felt tired when his driver came to take him to his branch line.

He huffed and puffed as he pulled Annie and Clarabel, who seemed even heavier than usual. When he came to a steep hill he had to pull really hard as he rushed to reach the top as fast as he could.

Just then Thomas remembered what Edward had said in the shed the night before. Perhaps Edward was right, thought Thomas, and he slowed down just a little bit.

No one seemed to notice, and Thomas still got to the end of the line on time.

On the way back, going slower than usual, Thomas felt pleased. His work seemed even more enjoyable now that he had time to look around him. He even had time to say hello to the cows in the fields beside his line.

Thomas was puffing along happily when he looked up the line and saw something that made him gasp.

"Cinders and ashes!" he said.

Up ahead, at the junction where he was going to meet James, there was a truck on the line. One of its wheels had come off, and the vegetables it was taking to the market were everywhere. There were boxes and sacks and cabbages and carrots all over the place.

Thomas had to stop before he hit the truck! He braked as hard as he could. His brakes squealed as he went slower and slower, but the truck got closer and closer.

"Oh, my wheels and coupling rods!" said Thomas. "Will I be able to stop in time?"

With one last big effort, Thomas managed to stop. He was very close to the truck. "You stopped just in time, Thomas!" said his driver. "Well done! What a clever little engine you are!"

"Yes, well done, Thomas," said the driver of the truck. "If you hadn't stopped in time there could have been a nasty accident." The passengers all leaned out of the windows and cheered and clapped.

That night, back in the shed, Thomas couldn't wait to tell his friends all about his exciting day. The other engines were as proud of Thomas as his driver was.

"Well done," said Edward. "You're a clever little engine."

"Thank you, Edward," said Thomas. "You're a clever engine, too. You were right about rushing around and going too fast. I took your advice, and slowed down a bit. I don't know if I would have been able to stop if I'd been going as fast as usual. I might have banged into that truck and had an accident."

"Well, we're all very glad you didn't," said Edward. "You were a real hero today."

"And I learned a lesson as well," said Thomas. "You do know best, Edward!"

Count with Thomas

It was such a mess when the wheel came off the truck!
There were boxes and sacks and vegetables all over Thomas' line.
It's a good job he wasn't going too fast to stop in time.

Good old Thomas!

Find and count these things in the big picture.
Write the number in each box.

13

Thomas the Famous Engine

One day, Sir Topham Hatt, The Fat Controller, spoke to all the engines in the Big Station.

2. "John Fairley, a famous artist, is coming to the railway to paint one of the engines," he said.

3. Sir Topham said the painting would be put on show. Lots of people would see it.

4. All the engines secretly hoped that Mr Fairley would choose them. Being painted was a great honour.

5. The engines wondered what their painting would be like. Crowds of people would come and admire them.

6. "Mr Fairley could paint me as a hard-working little green engine," said Percy. "With my trucks."

7. James said, "I'm a Really Splendid Engine! How nice my red paint and shiny brass dome will look!"

8. "A painting of me steaming along, fast and powerful, would look fine," said Gordon, the Big Express.

9. Edward is an older engine. "It would be nice to be painted with one of the small engines," he said.

10. Henry is a proud engine. "Just think how smart my shiny green paint will look!" he said.

11. Thomas hoped that if he was chosen, he would be painted as a busy little engine.

12. **Mr Fairley** liked all the engines, but he could only paint one.
Which would it be?

13. "I'm going to paint Thomas," he said at last. "Because he is keen and busy – and has a cheeky face!"

14. Thomas was pleased.
Next day he stayed in the Big Station as the others steamed off for the day.

15. Percy was going to do Thomas' work. He was looking forward to working with Annie and Clarabel.

16. Mr Fairley told Thomas what to do. "Back a bit," he said. "Now, keep quite still. Don't move a buffer."

17. Thomas had to stay still for hours while Mr Fairley painted. He couldn't move at all. He felt fed up.

18. Thomas worried about his branch line. "I hope Percy meets up with Toby and Henrietta on time!" he said.

19. "Will Annie and Clarabel manage without me?" Thomas thought. He couldn't wait to get back to work.

20. It was a long, long, boring day for Thomas. He liked his painting but was glad when it was finished.

21. **In the shed that night** Thomas couldn't wait to hear what the other engines had been up to.

22. **But the others** wanted to hear about his day. "What was it like being painted?" asked Percy. "Good fun?"

23. "**It was all right,**" said Thomas. "But not half as much fun as working on my own branch line! Peep! Peep!"

Read with Thomas

"**I** have lots of friends on the railway.
This is a story about one of them. Read it yourself. There are little pictures in place of some words, to help you."

 has his own branch line.

One day The  brought a

new  to work on it.

Toby is a Tram Engine.

He has a  called Henrietta.

They take the 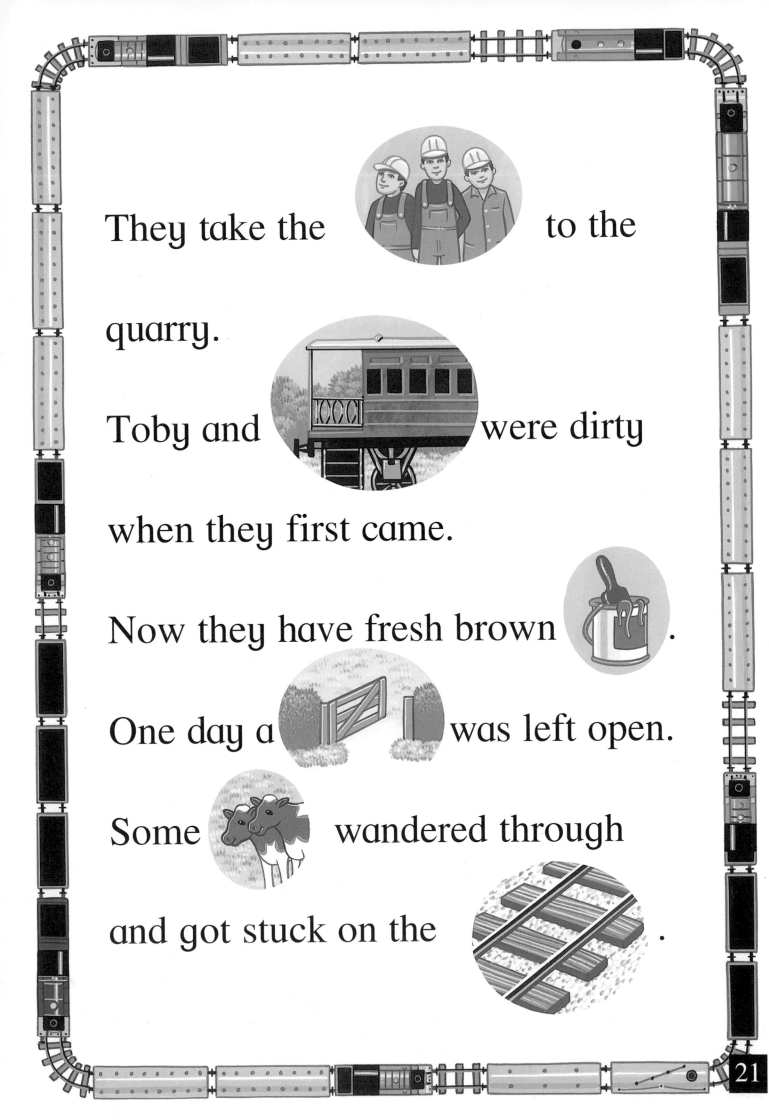 to the

quarry.

Toby and were dirty

when they first came.

Now they have fresh brown .

One day a was left open.

Some wandered through

and got stuck on the .

Along came Thomas. His  tried to shoo the cows away.

Thomas blew his  at them.

"Peep, peep!"

Then along came .

He has cowcatchers on the front.

He tried to move the  off the , but they would not go.

"I have to meet James," said  . "I'm late!"

Toby has a large, bright  .

He rang it extra loud.

"Ring, ding, ding!"

The  ran back to their  .

"Good old !"

said Thomas.

Double Trouble

It was a very special day at the railway.
A class of children from the local school were visiting the Big Station. Sir Topham Hatt, The Fat Controller, showed them around and told them all about how the railway works. Later, the children met some of the engines.

Two of the children were twins called David and Danny. They looked very alike, and wore the same clothes. Even their teacher wasn't sure which was David and which was Danny!

The twins were a bit naughty, and kept doing things they shouldn't. David looked inside some mail sacks.

"Don't do that, please, Danny!" said his teacher.

Danny tried to ride a mail truck like a scooter.

"Don't do that, David!" said The Fat Controller.

"I'm Danny, not David!" said Danny.

"And I'm David, not Danny!" said David. "It's not fair. People are always mixing us up. We keep getting blamed for things we didn't do."

"The twins can be a bit of a problem," the teacher told Sir Topham. "They don't like it when people get them mixed up. But it's so hard to tell them apart."

"Yes, David and Danny look exactly alike," said Sir Topham. "But lots of twins are like that."

"I know," said their teacher. "But David and Danny have never met another set of twins. Perhaps if they did they'd understand how difficult it is for people to tell them apart. They would understand how easy it is for people to get them mixed up."

Sir Topham Hatt felt sorry for the twins. Then he had an idea, and he asked Thomas to help him with a very special plan. A secret plan.

As soon as The Fat Controller had told him what to do, Thomas puffed happily out of the Big Station. He was very pleased to be helping with The Fat Controller's secret plan.

"Where are you going in such a hurry?" asked Percy, who was busy with the trucks in the yard.

"I can't tell you," said Thomas. "It's a secret! Peep, peep!"

Before long, Thomas chuffed back into the Big Station. This time, he wasn't on his own – he brought Donald and Douglas, and Bill and Ben, the two sets of twin engines, with him!

The Fat Controller introduced the twins to Donald and Douglas and Bill and Ben. "Would you like to help clean the twin engines?" he asked.

"Yes, please!" said David.

"Yes, please!" said Danny.

"Right," said The Fat Controller. "I want you to polish Douglas' funnel and clean Donald's buffers. When you've finished that, you can wash Ben's dome and polish Bill's wheels."

The twins soon got mixed up.

"Which is Bill?" asked David.

"Is this one Ben?" said Danny. "They look just the same."

The Fat Controller had put covers over the engines' name and number plates, so David and Danny couldn't see them.

The twins got even more mixed up.

"Which is Donald and which is Douglas?" said Danny.

"How can we tell which engine is which?" said David.

The twin engines enjoyed the joke, and Sir Topham laughed.
"It's very difficult to tell the difference between Douglas and Donald and Bill and Ben, isn't it?" he said. "We have the same trouble telling you two apart! You look just the same, too!"

Sir Topham took the covers off the engines' name and number plates.

"Look," he said. "This is how we tell our twin engines apart. They each have special nameplates and Donald and Douglas also have number plates, so we always know which is which."

"That's what we need," said David. "Nameplates."

Their teacher laughed. "Yes, they would be very useful!" she said.

A few days after the children's day at the railway, The Fat Controller asked the twins to visit him again.

David and Danny were very pleased.

When they got there, all the engines were in the Big Station. Donald and Douglas and Bill and Ben were at the front, nearest to the platform. They watched as Sir Topham gave each of the twins a little box.

David opened his box. "It's a badge," he said. "And it's got my name on it."

Danny opened his box. "I've got a badge with my name on it, too," he said. "It's just like the ones the twin engines have, but smaller."

"Now we know who's who," said The Fat Controller. "You are the only children to have nameplates like the engines."

"Thank you," said David. "It's fun being a twin sometimes."

"Yes, it is," said Danny.

The twin engines agreed.

"Peep, peep!" said Donald and Douglas.
"Pip, pip!" said Bill and Ben.

Twin Engines Game

One day the twin engines, Bill and Ben, decided to have a race. Which of the twins will be first to reach the Big Station?

Play the game with a friend.
One of you plays for Bill.
The other plays for Ben.

You need a die and a counter each.
Take turns to shake the die.
Move along the track the number on the die.
If you shake 2, move 2 places, and so on.

If you land on a red flag, miss a turn.
If you land on a green flag, have an extra throw.

The first to get to the Big Station wins the race!

START

30

FINISH

Competition Time

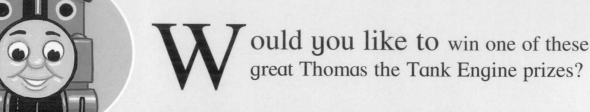

Would you like to win one of these great Thomas the Tank Engine prizes?

All you have to do is answer this question:

What is the title of the first story in the annual?

Then you could win a super

Thomas the Tank Engine Activity Train and Carriages.

It's a push-along train and art centre all rolled into one!

The train includes: chunky crayons and pencils, a self-inking roller stamper with three roller options, six paint pots and a brush, and a hidden pencil sharpener in the rear buffers! Peep! Peep!

There are also 50 runners-up prizes of **6 Chunky Crayons** to colour your favourite Thomas pictures!

Write your entry on a postcard, or on the back of a sealed envelope.

There are two things you must remember to tell us:

1. Your answer to the question.   2. Your name, age and address.

Send your entry to : Thomas the Tank Engine & Friends Annual Competition, Egmont World Limited, Deanway Technology Centre, Wilmslow Road, Handforth, Cheshire SK9 3FB.

The closing date is **Friday 14th January 2000**

The Thomas Train & Carriages & The Chunky Crayons are part of a wide range of award winning Thomas the Tank Engine Creative Play items from Chelful.

Details of the range and stockists available from the Chelful Customer Hotline 01332 297363

Buzzing Bees!

O ne summer evening, Thomas had finished work on his branch line. He had had a busy day, but he didn't mind; Thomas likes being busy. He enjoys huffing and chuffing about up and down his line.

He puffed happily back along the track towards the yard and slowed down to say hello to the sheep on Farmer Mills' farm.

'Buzz, buzz!' Suddenly, there were bees everywhere. They buzzed angrily around Thomas' funnel, 'buzz, buzz, buzz!'

They buzzed around Thomas' coaches, Annie and Clarabel, too, and flew in and out of their open windows.

Thomas was annoyed. "Peep, peep!" he said. "Go away! Buzz off!"

Those bees were a real nuisance! They buzzed around all the engines as they steamed past that same part of the track.

That night, in the shed they shared, the engines talked about the bees.

"Some of them flew right down into my funnel," said Henry. "I had to blow really hard to get them out."

Even Gordon, the senior engine, and the biggest and most powerful engine, had been bothered by the bees. "They were everywhere!" he said. "All that buzzing was very annoying. Poop, poop!"

The next morning, when Thomas chugged back along the line, the bees were still there, buzzing around angrily.

When Thomas' driver saw Farmer Mills waving to him from the side of the track, he put on the brakes, and Thomas stopped. The bees flew round and round his funnel.

'Buzz, buzz!' They sounded very angry indeed.

"What's wrong with you?" said Thomas. "Buzz off, you silly, noisy bees!"

"Where have all these bees come from, Farmer Mills?" asked Thomas' driver.

"They're mine," said Farmer Mills. "I keep them in that row of hives over there. I collect their honey and put it in jars to sell. The bees are usually very quiet and happy, but they are very worried and angry just now because a large tree branch fell on to their hives and damaged them. The bees all flew out of the hives and are in a bit of a panic. That's why they sound so angry! I've tried to calm them down and get them into the new hives I've made for them, but they are very frightened, and they won't go in. That's why they are buzzing around everywhere. They're upset."

Thomas' driver nodded, and took off his cap to wave it at the bees that buzzed and hummed around his head.

"The bees are a nuisance," he said. "Our passengers have been complaining about them. They even buzzed around The Fat Controller's top hat. He wasn't very pleased."

"I know," said Farmer Mills. "But I don't know what to do. I keep the bees calm and happy in the same way that all bee-keepers do. I puff some smoke into the hives to keep them quiet, but the machine that I use to make the smoke was broken when the tree branch fell on the hives. Without it, I can't make smoke to calm the bees."

Thomas had an idea of how he could help Farmer Mills.

Later, when he was back in the yard, Thomas went to find Henry, the big green number 3 engine.

"Are those bees still causing trouble on the line?" asked Henry, who was a bit nervous, and didn't like them buzzing around him.

"Yes, they are," said Thomas. "I think I know how to stop them, but I need your help." Thomas told Henry what Farmer Mills had said. "Farmer Mills needs smoke – lots and lots of it!" said Thomas. "You're good at making smoke, aren't you, Henry? Will you come with me to the farm and make lots of smoke to calm the bees?"

Henry was fed up with the bees buzzing around, so he agreed to help.

Henry and Thomas puffed off along the line again and stopped close to the beehives. Henry puffed and puffed, working hard to blow out as much smoke as he could. Soon, there was smoke everywhere, and it had an amazing effect on the bees! As they flew through the smoke, the bees slowed down, and were much quieter. Soon their angry buzz, buzz, buzzing stopped and they just hummed quietly.

"Well done, Henry!" said Farmer Mills. "Thank you, Thomas!"

Farmer Mills soon got all the bees safely into the new hives. They were still making a noise, but they didn't sound angry now. Instead, the bees made a low, happy humming noise.

"That means they feel safe and happy again," Farmer Mills told Thomas and Henry. "They don't feel frightened and angry any more."

Thanks to Thomas and Henry, everyone was happy. Farmer Mills was happy, the engines and the railway passengers were happy, and Sir Topham Hatt was happy.

Best of all, the bees were happy. As soon as they had settled into their new hives they set about doing what bees do best – making lots and lots of lovely yellow honey.

A few days later the engine drivers and firemen felt happy too, when Farmer Mills went to visit them at the Big Station. He brought some jars of golden honey to say thank you for their help.

"Thank you for your good idea, Thomas!" said Farmer Mills.

"Peep, peep!" said Thomas, who is always glad to help.

"Thank you, Henry, for making all that smoke!" said Farmer Mills.

Henry felt proud. He blew out a little puff of smoke.

"Poop, poop!" he said happily.

Count with Henry

Henry was pleased that he was able to help stop the bees buzzing around. His puffs of smoke made the bees quiet and calm again.

"Now buzz off back to your new hives!" said Henry.

"Poop, poop!"

Find and count these things in the big picture.
Write the number in each box.

Make a Special Millennium Door Hanger

The year 2000 is a very special one. Why not make this year 2000 door hanger? You can hang it on the door when you are reading your Thomas Annual and don't want to be disturbed!

You need:
card
pencil
ruler
tracing paper
safety scissors
felt-tip pens

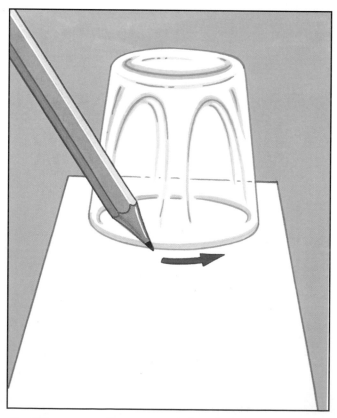

1. Ask a grown-up to help you measure and cut out a strip of card about 24cm long and 10cm wide.

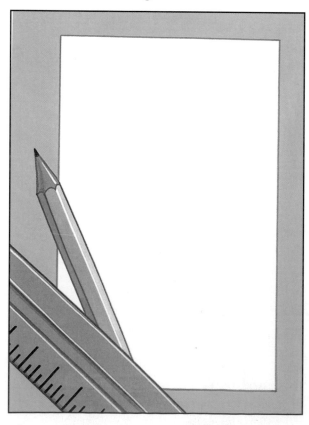

2. Place a glass upside down in the middle of the card, near the top. Draw round the glass.

3. Start to cut into the card from the edge until you meet the drawn circle. Cut the circle out and then cut back to the same edge you started from.

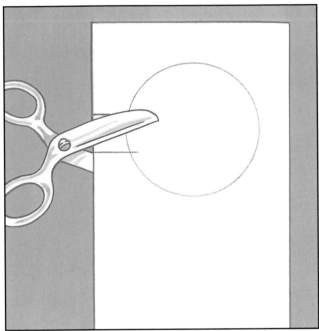

4. Trace this drawing of Thomas at the bottom of your hanger, remembering to leave room for your message.

5. Write the number 2000 at the top of the hanger for the Millennium. Colour your hanger.

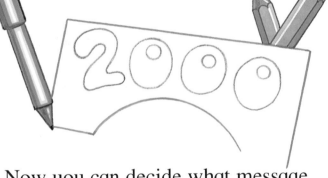

Now you can decide what message you would like – here are a few!

DO NOT DISTURB!
QUIET!
PLEASE KNOCK!
PEEP! PEEP!
THE FAT CONTROLLER'S OFFICE
THE BIG STATION

Happy reading!

Copy Colour with Thomas

Thomas is very busy today at the Big Station. Copy the colours from the scene opposite to finish off this picture.

How many parcels can you see hidden in this picture?

I can see ⟨9⟩ parcels in each picture.

The Flood

It had been raining for days and days on the Island of Sodor. The sky was dark and grey and a cold wind blew. The ground was wet and muddy, and covered in puddles. Rain dripped from the leaves on the trees.

The bad weather made everyone feel miserable. The drivers and firemen didn't like working in wet weather, and the passengers wanted to stay at home where it was warm and dry.

Every evening, when the engines chuffed into their shed for the night, they were wet. Water dripped from their domes and funnels and buffers, and ran down their paintwork. It made them feel cold and damp.

All the engines were fed up with the rain, but Henry, the long, fast number 3 engine, was especially miserable. He doesn't like the rain because he is very proud of his shiny green paint, and gets upset when it gets wet and messy.

"Oh, just look at my paintwork," said Henry sadly. "I usually look smart and neat, but now I look messy. I do wish the rain would stop!"

But the rain did not stop.

Big drops drummed and rattled on the roof of the engine shed all night long. The noise kept waking the engines, and when Henry did get to sleep, he had a bad dream about his paintwork being dull and patchy.

James, the red number 5 engine, had a bad dream, too. The rain made his shiny brass dome all dull and brown and rusty. He didn't look like a Really Splendid Engine now!

It was still raining when Thomas chuffed out of the shed and hurried along to his branch line the next morning. The river that runs by the side of his line was swollen with rainwater. The river was running really fast, and muddy water was lapping and slapping against the banks.

"Oh, dear," said Thomas' driver when he saw the river. "This is a big problem. If the rain doesn't stop soon, the water will get higher and higher. The river will burst its banks, and the fields along the line will all be flooded. The cows and sheep will be in danger. The station will be flooded, too, and that means that we won't be able to look after our passengers. We won't be able to deliver goods, either. And we won't be able to help get the men to work at the quarry."

Thomas and his driver hurried back to the Big Station as fast as they could. Thomas' driver told Sir Topham Hatt, The Fat Controller, about the river.

"You're right to be worried," said Sir Topham. "This is very serious, but I know what to do. If we all work hard, I think we can stop the flood and save Thomas' branch line."

Sir Topham had all the engines and their drivers brought to the Big Station. "This is an emergency," he told them. "There is a real danger that Thomas' branch line will be flooded. But if we all work together, I think we can stop the water doing any damage. Now listen carefully, this is what I want you to do …"

A few minutes later, all the engines set off, huffing and chuffing and puffing, steaming down towards the harbour as fast as they could. They stopped on the part of the track that ran along the beach. There, all the men jumped off, and were soon busy with shovels, filling sacks and old mailbags with sand.

The drivers and firemen dragged the heavy sacks of sand back to where the engines were waiting. As soon as the coaches were packed with sandbags, the engines set off, one by one, and steamed off as fast as they could to Thomas' branch line.

Near the station the men jumped off the engines again, and pulled and dragged the sacks of sand to the river bank. They piled them up, higher and higher, to keep the water in the river and stop it spilling over the banks and flooding on to the land.

The engines had a long, long day and worked very hard, but they were all glad to help, even Henry! He still didn't like getting his smart green paintwork wet, but he knew how serious a flood would be for Thomas' branch line and the whole railway.

Sir Topham Hatt and all the railway workers worked hard, too. At the end of the day, just as it was starting to get dark, he called all the engines together. It was still raining. "Well done, everyone," he said. "Thanks to all your hard work, I think Thomas' branch line is safe. The sandbags are holding the water back. It will be dark soon, so there's nothing else we can do tonight. Let's just hope the rain stops."

Back in the engine shed, the men wiped the engines to dry them, then went home for a well-earned rest.

The engines were still worried that the branch line might be flooded if the river burst its banks, but they had done all they could to stop it. Thomas listened, worrying, as the rain still rattled and drummed on the shed roof, but at last even he fell asleep, tired out.

Thomas was the last engine to go to sleep, and the first to wake up again next morning.

He blinked, wide awake right away. Something was different, but what was it?

Thomas listened hard. "Peep, peep!" he whistled happily. "Wake up, Edward! Wake up, Henry and James! Wake up, Gordon! You too, Percy!"

"What is it?" asked Percy, who was still tired after all his hard work the day before.

"Listen!" said Thomas. "It's the rain. The rain has stopped! The river won't break its banks and flood the fields and the railway track. My branch line is safe!"

The engines all felt very pleased.

Thomas yawned sleepily. "I'm still a bit tired," he said. "I hope we aren't as busy today as we were yesterday. It was very hard work bringing all those sandbags from the beach. I think we deserve a rest."

Edward smiled at Thomas. "I don't think we'll get a rest today, Thomas," he said. "Now that the rain has stopped, the water in the river will go down again – and we'll have to take all those sacks of sand back to the beach."

"Oh, no!" said Thomas. "Peep, peep!" But his branch line was safe, so he didn't mind really.

Race to the River Game

All the engines helped when Thomas' branch line was in danger of being flooded. As soon as the men had loaded the engines with bags of sand, they steamed off for the river. Thomas and Percy, the smallest engines, were the first to set off. They chuffed and puffed along as fast as they could.

Which engine got to the river first, Thomas or Percy?
Play this game to find out.
You need a die, 2 counters, and a friend to play with. Choose to be Thomas or Percy.
Take turns to throw the die.
Move along the track the number you score.
If you score 3, move 3 spaces, and so on.

If you land in a puddle, go back 3 spaces.
If you land in some mud, miss a turn.

The first to reach the river is the winner. Will it be Thomas or Percy?

FINISH

51

Star Engines

O ne day Sir Topham Hatt, The Fat Controller, had some very exciting news for the engines.

2. "A television company is going to use the railway to make a film," he told them.

3. "The film is about some children who become very special friends with the engines."

4. "Three engines will be chosen to be in the film," said Sir Topham. "They will be Star Engines!"

5. "Peep, peep!" said Thomas. "Which three engines will it be?" "Wait and see," said Sir Topham.

6. That night, in the engine shed, the engines talked about the film. Who would be chosen to be in it?

7. James, who thinks he's a Really Splendid Engine, thought he would be one of the stars.

8. **So did Henry,** the long, fast number 3 engine, who is very proud of his shiny green paint.

9. **Gordon said** he would be the third engine. "We are the largest engines, after all," he boasted.

10. **"I do hope** you are chosen for the film," said kind old Edward, the blue engine.

11. **"So do I,"** said young Percy, who is quite happy puffing around the yard with the trucks.

12. Thomas wanted to be in the film, but he thought the television people would choose the larger engines.

13. "I hope you enjoy making the film," he told them. "Do you think I can come and watch?"

14. The next day Henry, Gordon and James went to the Big Station to meet the TV people.

15. "Henry, Gordon and James are really fine engines," the man in charge of the film told Sir Topham.

16. "But they are rather large," he said. "Are there any other engines? Smaller ones?"

17. "Yes," said Sir Topham, and he sent for his smaller engines, Thomas, Percy and Toby.

18. "They are just the right size!" said the man when he saw them.

19. The smaller engines really enjoyed being in the film. Acting was lots and lots of fun!

20. **When the film** was finished, they couldn't wait to tell the larger engines all about it.

21. **Thomas** felt especially pleased with himself. He liked the idea of being a special Star Engine.

22. **"What happens** in the film?" asked Henry. "I'm not allowed to say," said Thomas importantly.

23. **"Why don't you ask** The Fat Controller to let you watch us on his TV," he said cheekily. "Peep! Peep!"

Read with Thomas

" **R**ead this story yourself.
There are little pictures in place
of some words to help you."

One day some arrived at the Big

 . There were **6** of them.

"They are 'thank you' cards from

 . It's polite to send a

when someone has helped you,"

said  .

"The first card says it is for the big

 engine."

"It's for me! It's from the 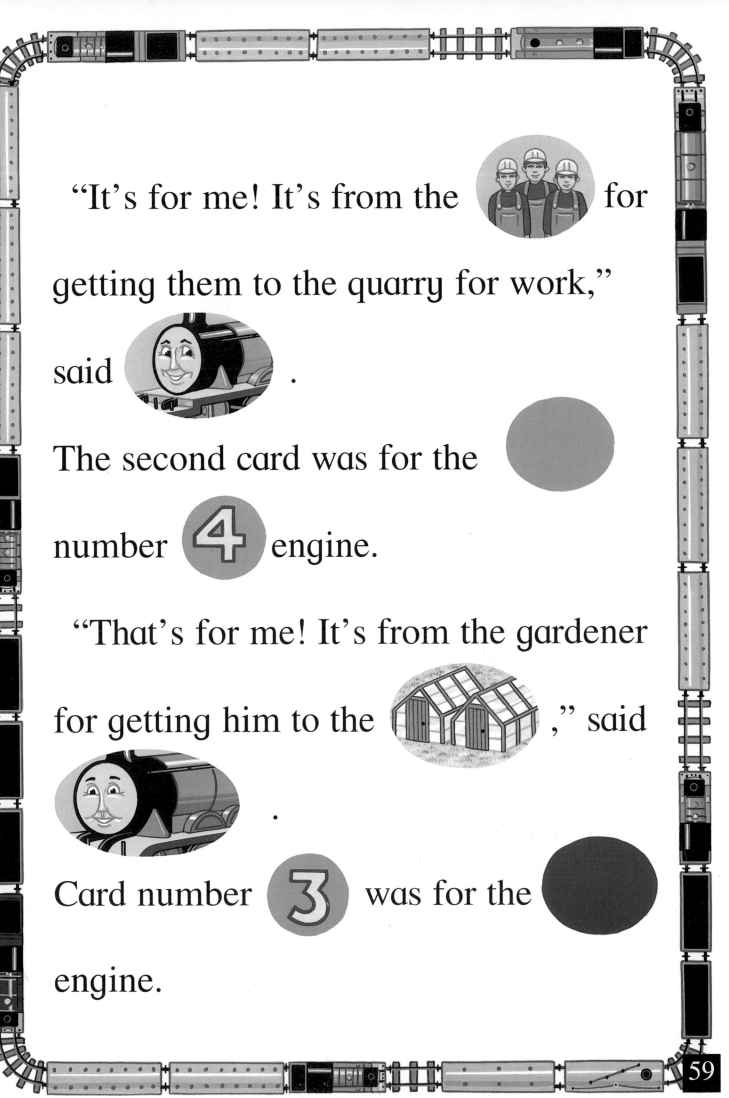 for

getting them to the quarry for work,"

said   .

The second card was for the

number 4 engine.

"That's for me! It's from the gardener

for getting him to the   ," said

          .

Card number 3 was for the

engine.

"I'm the only red engine. It's for me!

It's from the baker for getting him to

the 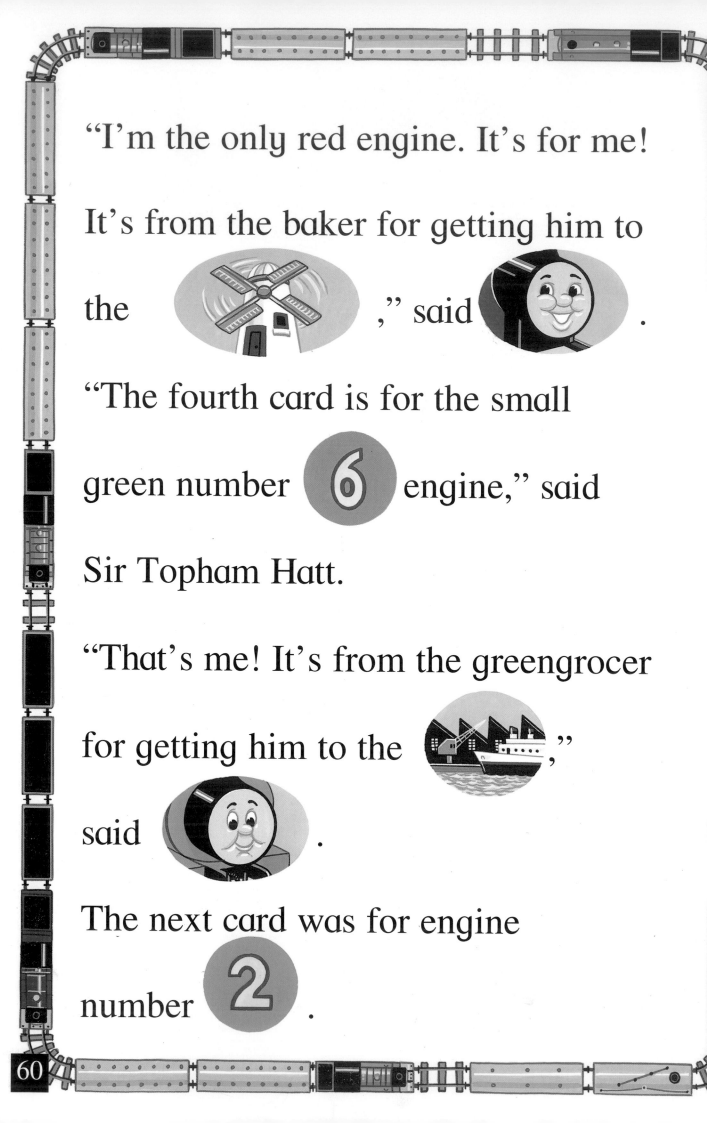 ," said .

"The fourth card is for the small

green number 6 engine," said

Sir Topham Hatt.

"That's me! It's from the greengrocer

for getting him to the ,"

said .

The next card was for engine

number 2 .

It was for 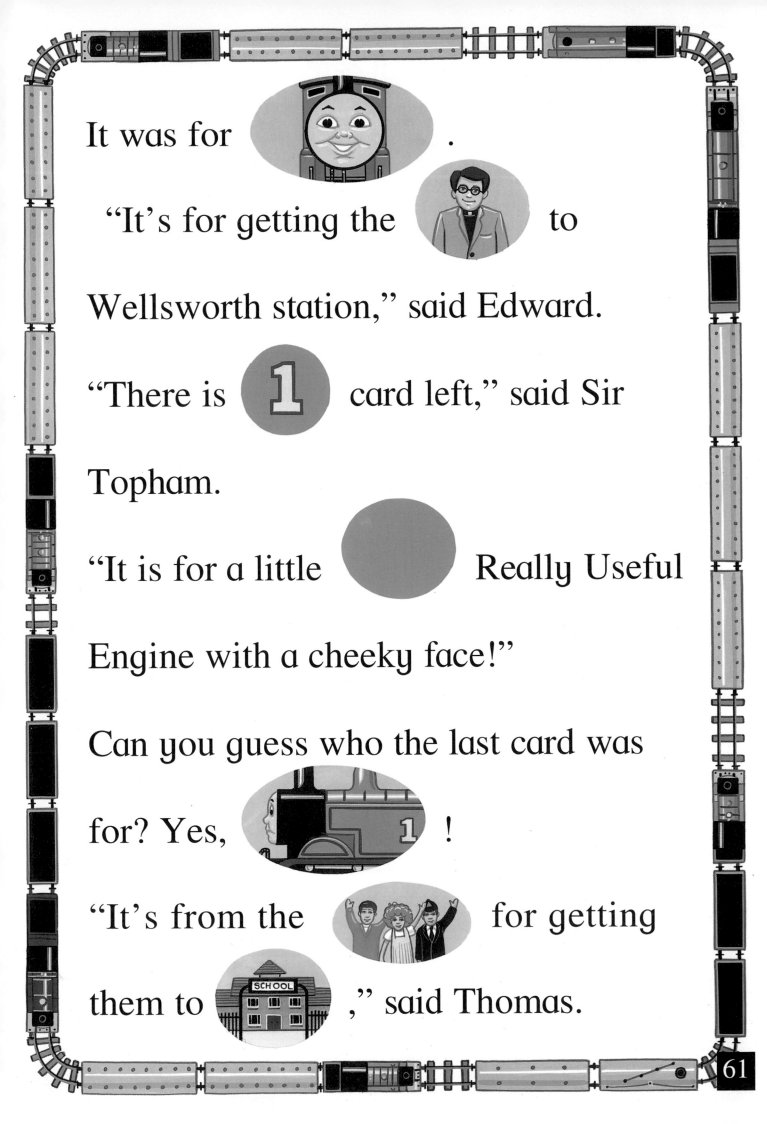 .

"It's for getting the 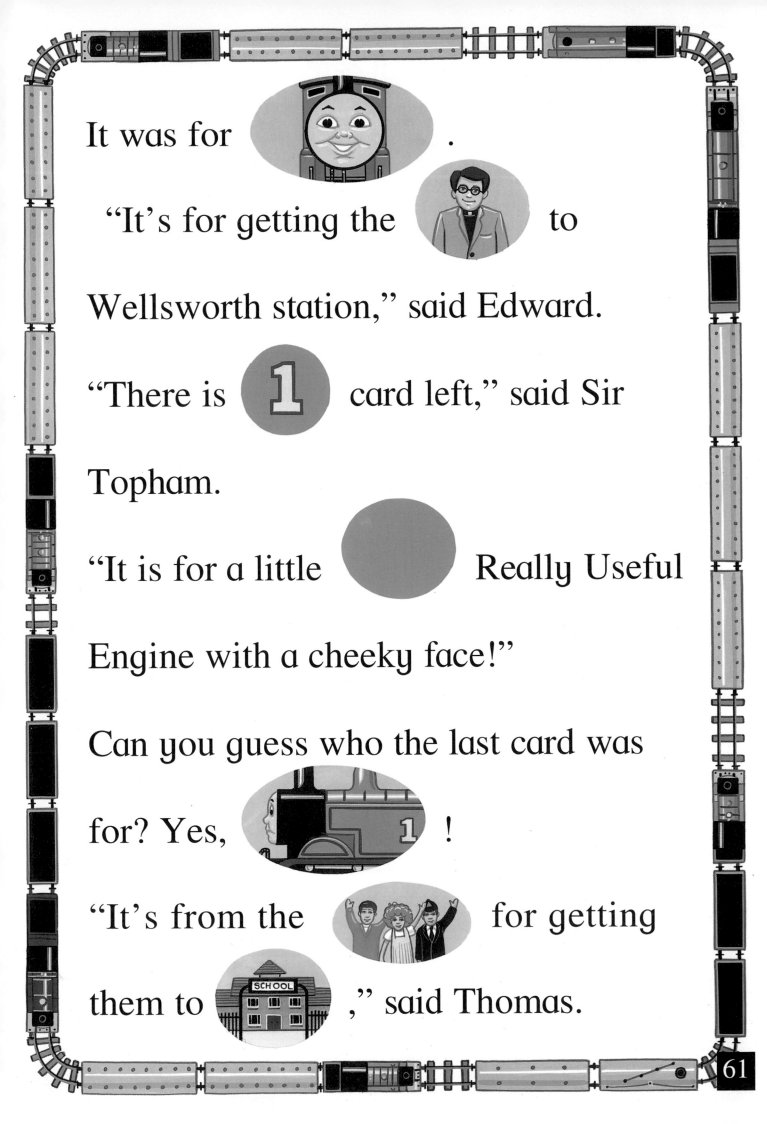 to

Wellsworth station," said Edward.

"There is 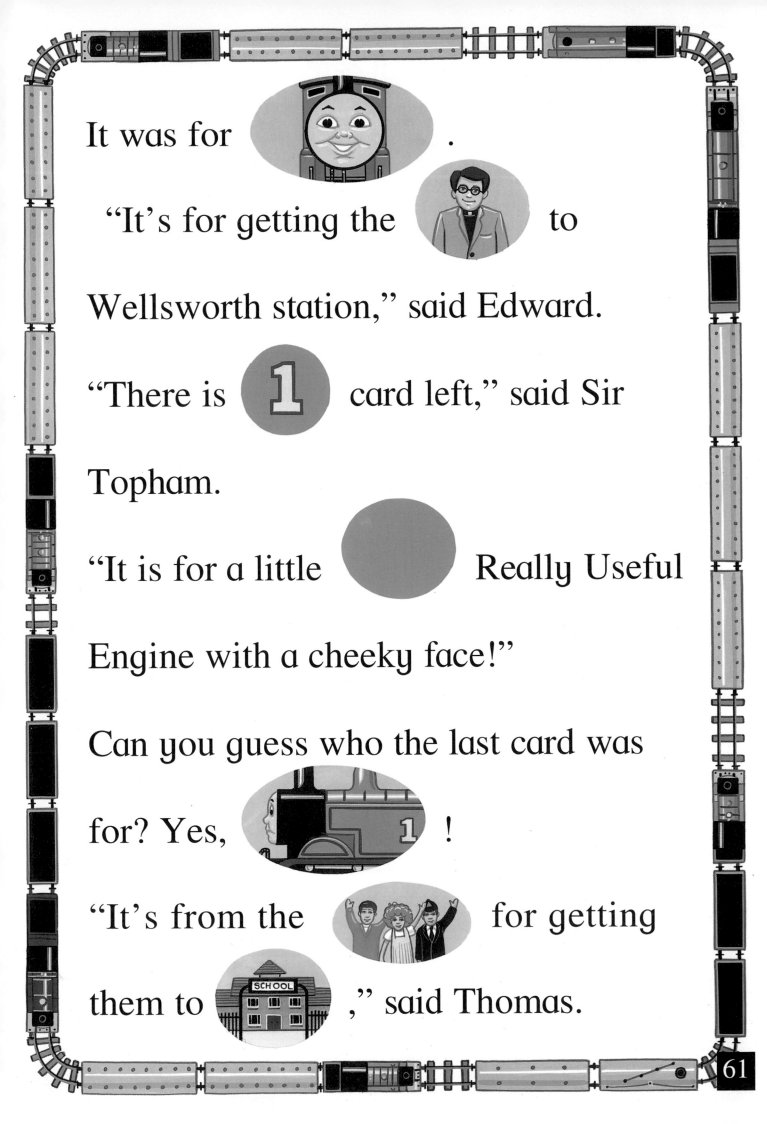 card left," said Sir

Topham.

"It is for a little 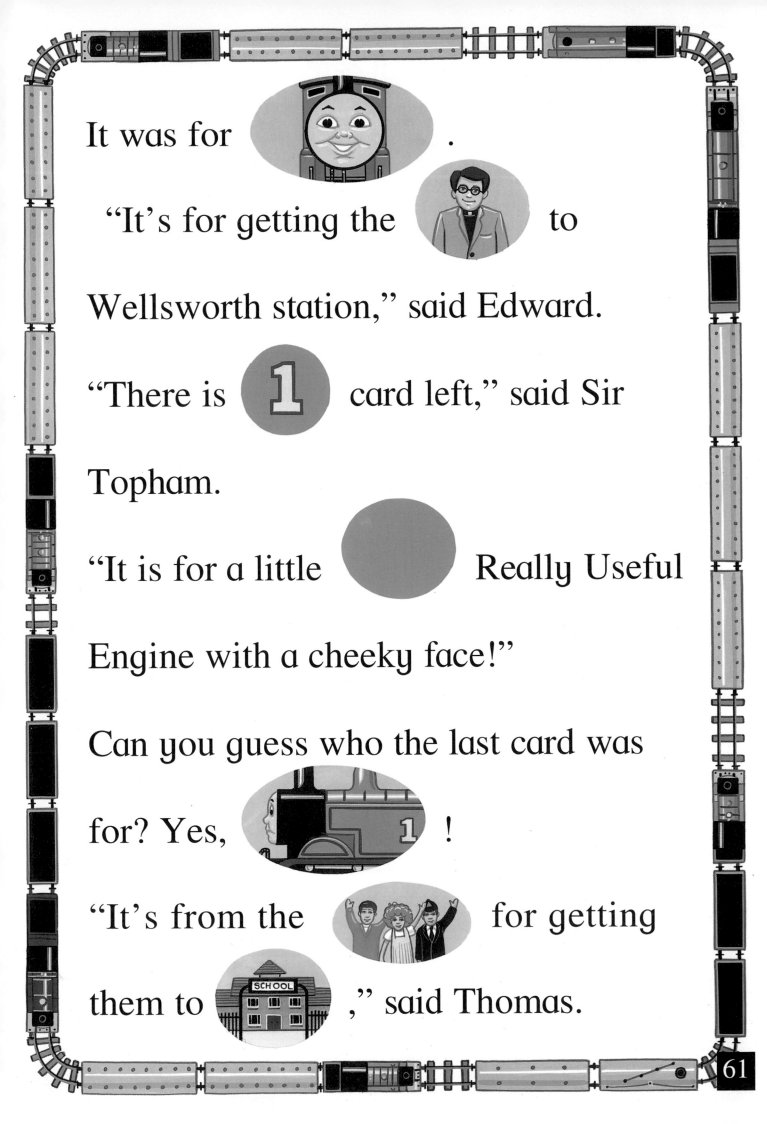 Really Useful

Engine with a cheeky face!"

Can you guess who the last card was

for? Yes, 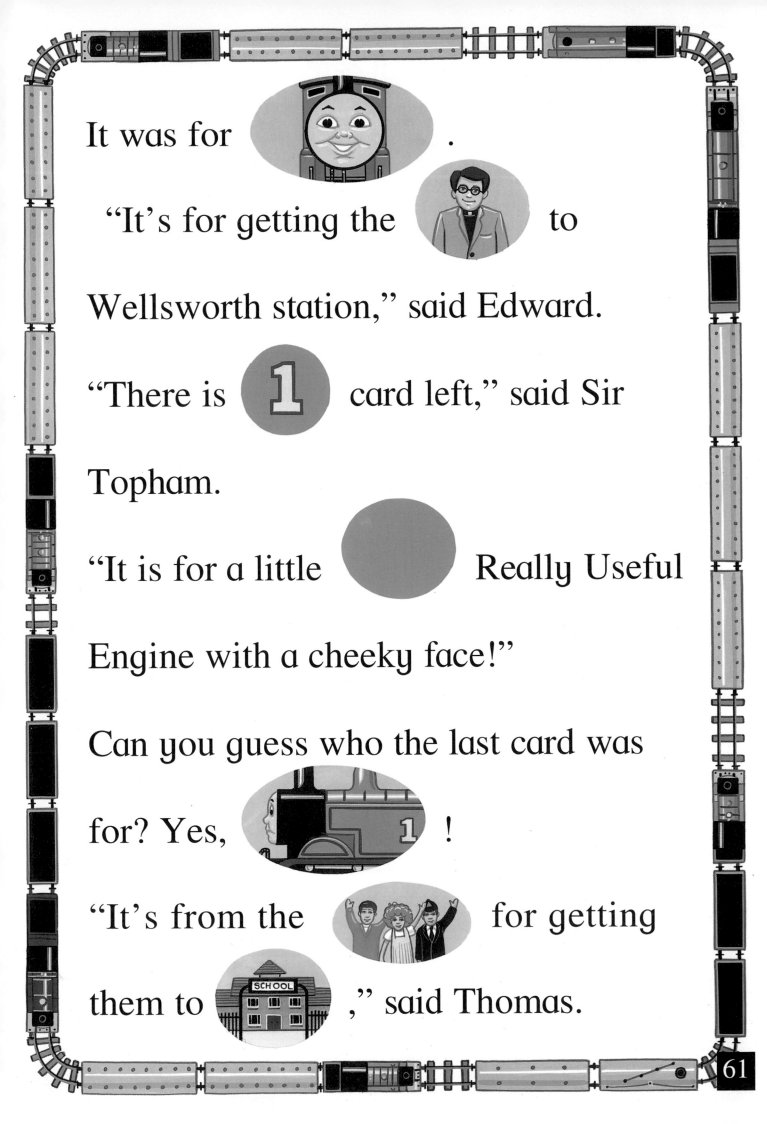 !

"It's from the 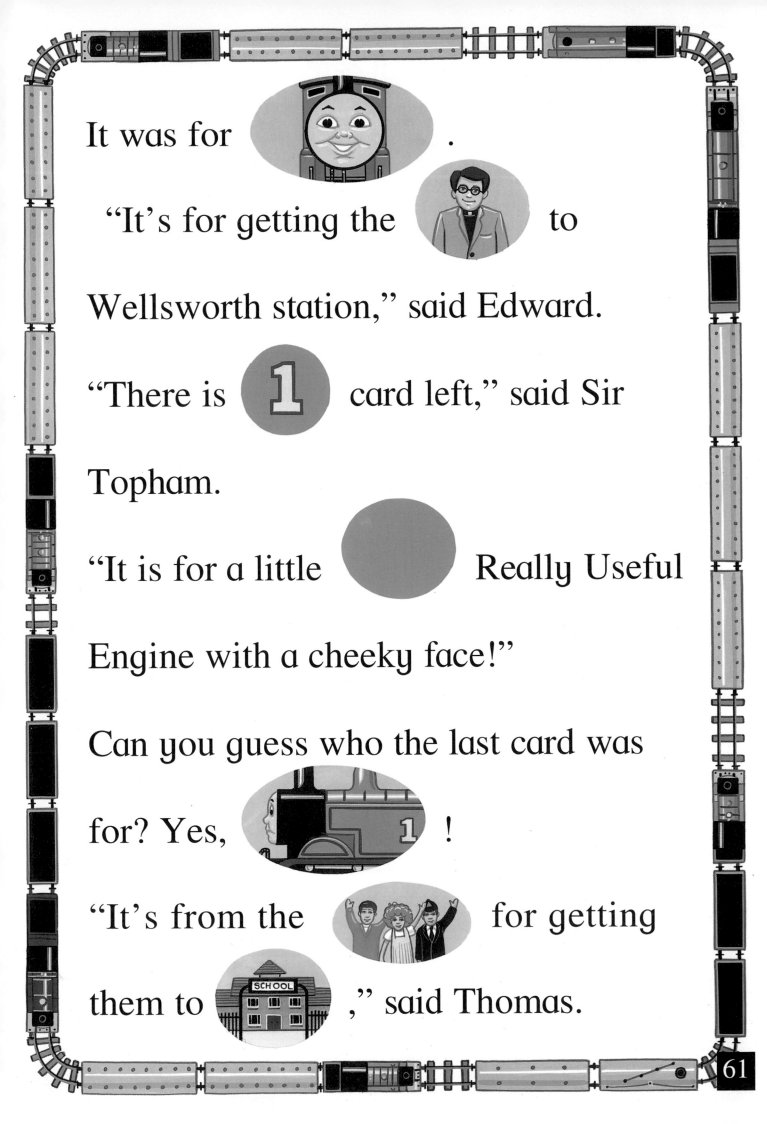 for getting

them to 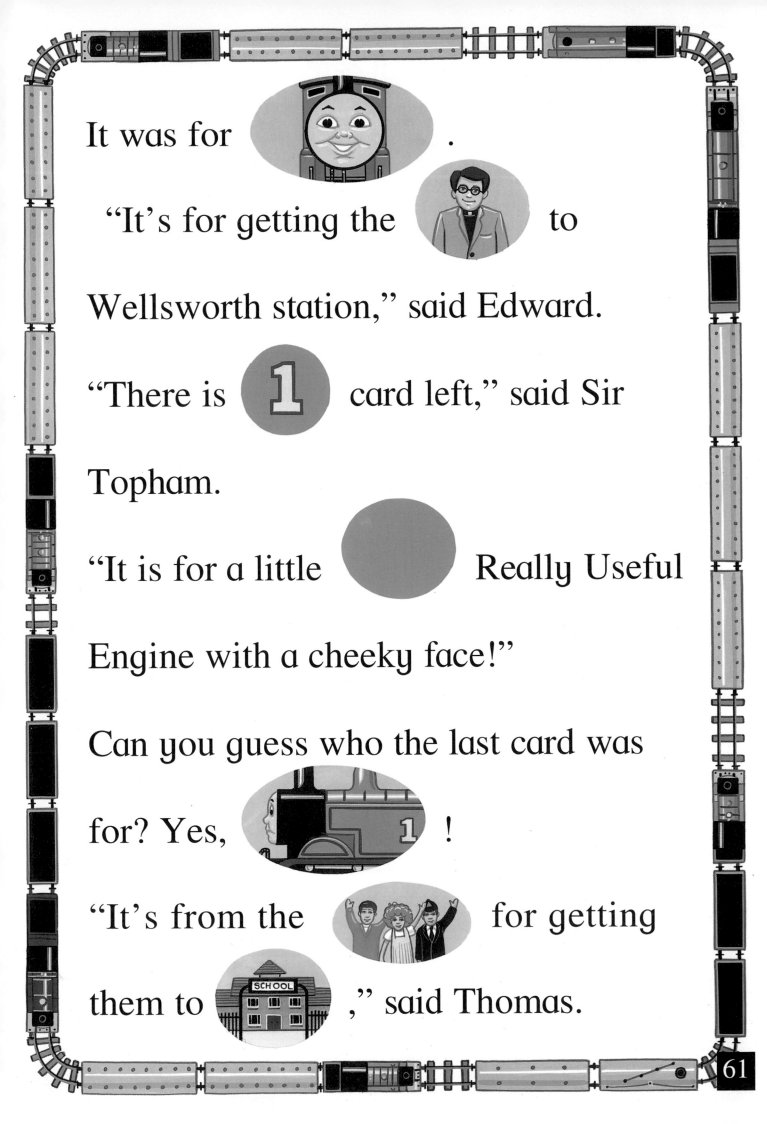 ," said Thomas.

GREAT PRIZE DRAW!

PEEP! PEEP!

Sir Topham Hatt here...
Are you a loyal friend of
my Number One
Engine? Then you'll
love The Thomas Club...

During the course of the year members receive:

- Fabulous Welcome Pack crammed with Thomas goodies for you to enjoy.
- Your very own birthday card **and** a Christmas card from Thomas
- One copy of the Club newsletter & The Thomas Catalogue, your guide to a fantastic range of Thomas goodies
- And the chance to submit four drawings a year to Sir Topham Hatt, who will stamp them and return them to you with a special message (please note: a stamped addressed envelope is required with each submission)

FANTASTIC WELCOME PACK!

T-Shirt £4.99!

GREAT PRIZE DRAW!

Win a Thomas the Tank Engine Ticket Office

10 lucky winners will be drawn at random to each receive an Absolutely Splendid Thomas The Tank Engine Ticket Office. Be your very own Station Master with play money, lost property compartment, timetable and pricelist, note pads and electronic sounds. You can also attach your Thomas track to the Ticket Office. And don't worry, if you are not a winner, the playset along with the complete range of Ertl trains are available from The Thomas Catalogue & most good toy retailers.

Everyone who is a Thomas Club member on the 14/1/2000 will be automatically entered into the draw so if you are not already one of Thomas' most loyal friends, don't delay, sign up today.

Rules:
1. 10 winners will be chosen at random and will be notified by post.
2. No purchase necessary. To enter without enrolling in The Thomas Club, send child's name, age and address and parents name on a postcard marked "TT2000 Draw" to , PO Box 142, Horsham, RH13 5FJ. Entries limited to one per person. Closing date 14/1/2000
3. No correspondence will be entered into.
4. A list of winners will be made available on request from Robell Media Promotions Ltd, PO Box 142, Horsham, RH13 5FJ after 14/2/2000. S.A.E. required.
5. Prize content may be varied subject to availability.

(Track and diecast engines and figures not included)

Thomas would love to welcome you aboard. So don't miss out on the fun - enrol today!

To join The Thomas Club, return the coupon to: The Thomas Club, Island of Sodor, PO Box 142, Horsham RH13 5FJ. Credit card customers may call 01403 273471 or fax 01403 261555.

© Britt Allcroft (Thomas) Limited 1999.

To be completed by an adult

Please enrol the following in The Thomas Club at £10.72 (£9.99 + 73p postage)

Member's Name:_____ Address:_____
_____
_____ Post Code:_____ Date of birth:___/___/___
Your Name:_____ Address (if different):_____
_____ Post Code:_____
Name of member's parent or guardian (if not you):_____
❏ Please enter me in the prize draw.
❏ Please also send a Club T-Shirt at £4.99. Size: __ age 3-4 __ age 5-6 __ age 7-8.
Total amount due: £_____ (£10.72 per membership, £4.99 per T-Shirt)
❏ I enclose a cheque or postal order payable to The Thomas Club
❏ Please charge my MasterCard/ Visa account.
Card number: ☐☐☐☐☐☐☐☐☐☐☐☐☐☐☐☐☐☐ Expiry Date: ___/___

Data Protection Act: If you do **not** wish to receive other family offers from us or companies we recommend, please tick this box ❏